PRIMARY DRIVE

Siddharth Khare

New Delhi • London

BLUEROSE PUBLISHERS
India | U.K.

Copyright © Siddharth Khare 2024

All rights reserved by author. No part of this publication may be reproduced, stored in a retrieval system or transmitted in any form or by any means, electronic, mechanical, photocopying, recording or otherwise, without the prior permission of the author. Although every precaution has been taken to verify the accuracy of the information contained herein, the publisher assumes no responsibility for any errors or omissions. No liability is assumed for damages that may result from the use of information contained within.

BlueRose Publishers takes no responsibility for any damages, losses, or liabilities that may arise from the use or misuse of the information, products, or services provided in this publication.

For permissions requests or inquiries regarding this publication, please contact:

BLUEROSE PUBLISHERS
www.BlueRoseONE.com
info@bluerosepublishers.com
+91 8882 898 898
+4407342408967

ISBN: 978-93-5989-328-0

Cover design: Devahuti
Typesetting: Pooja Sharma

First Edition: February 2024

Rohan could not believe he hit her, he never thought he was capable of hitting anyone. Before that moment he had never even raised his voice but that day he crossed a line – a line which was tormenting him. A part of his mind said, "it's alright, it doesn't matter" while the other part quickly retorted, "this shows the kind of man you are". He realized he was not even angry at her, yet he did what he did. It was against everything he believed, he downloaded anger from somewhere else to someone else. He knew there was no way to make up for this; there were no scars, physical or emotional. Still, he could not undo what he had done. Even if he removed the memory of this from his robot, whom he had hit, he will always remember it.

That night was even more sleepless than usual for him; he hardly slept for a couple of hours. Waking up, he hoped that events from the last night would not torment him today. As his robot brought him breakfast, memories from the night before flooded back. Unable to make eye contact with her, he decided to shut her down and get ready for his work. He couldn't let his personal struggles impact his work.

Rohan worked as a senior artificial intelligence engineer at Geouniverse. He worked just enough to keep himself out of focus, neither in good grace nor in bad. His company had been through many changes over the last few years, there was a period when it seemed people had lost interest in AI; visionaries believed that AI couldn't solve new problems anymore and, like the dot-com bubble of the late 90s AI would fall too. And it did fall to a certain extent but then revived again by newer advancements.

Rohan quickly got ready, took a seat at the back of his car, and let the car drive him to his office. Along the way, he noticed the billboards advertising new robots which he knew was the same old software in new packaging. He observed a couple of shops selling new robots and re-purposing the old ones. He began wondering about the changes that the AI industry has been through over the last few years.

Facial recognition and automated cars were perfected a while back. Initially mechanical robots began working in offices for various tasks. Over time, they found their way into homes, and eventually, they started handling more complex jobs as well. With advancements in technology, robots now have the look and feel of humans, and their movements have been perfected as well, now robots can do human-dance as well. With tissue-like bodies and human-like movements robots were widely used for sexual pleasure, it turned out to be relatively easy to sexually gratify humans.

After analyzing data from the abundantly available adult content and from individuals willingly congregating in front of numerous cameras and motion sensor devices, machines have tons of data to identify the responses needed by humans. A lot of these individuals believed it to be an achievement that robots are going to mimic their actions while pleasing other people. They didn't realize that they were being analyzed to comprehend diverse human needs.

The AI industry didn't just invite potentially good performers but all kinds of people so that they can understand the full spectrum of human needs. Robots, equipped with these insights, can identify the sexual needs of their individual owners. They also have customizable settings such as noise, roughness, age, preferences, and more.

There is still a black market where people can buy robots which can perform sexual acts deemed illegal by the governments.

The newer challenges that the AI industry was working on, was the humans' need for interaction. It's not that robots cannot communicate, with the advancements in AI and natural language processing, robots can read, write, and speak like humans. Some of the books penned by robots but sold as written by humans have been bestsellers. There was a huge uproar once the truth came out in the open. Government had passed the law that there should be clear demarcation between humans and robots, an individual was not supposed to pass his or her robot as a person. It was mandated that all robots will be equipped with devices for easy detection. As a result people can use robots for sexual pleasure but cannot pass them as their girlfriend or boyfriend.

Experiments and studies by AI companies have revealed that people have no problem in being friends with robots, if they didn't know that they were interacting with robots. However, once the knowledge was out people were not interested in further interaction. This behavior was not observed in children, but the government had banned child-like robots. All robots were to be modeled both physically and mentally after adult human beings. AI companies were trying different ways to make people embrace robots as friends and companions so that they can sell newer and costlier robots. There were robots designed by AI companies to completely emulate humans. These robots can have dinner conversations, they can party, they can listen about the day at work. But after an initial spike in sales, these robots ultimately stayed on the shelf. AI companies recognized this as the next big market, understanding that whoever solved the problem of how robots can replace humans as friends, as companions, will win the race.

Rohan worked in one such AI company striving to replace humans as companions. Today he completed eleven years in the AI industry. Just before the incident of hitting his robot, he was sitting alone in a bar, after being dumped for the fifth time in the last two years. Despite this being his fifth relationship in that span, Rohan had harbored some hopes for this one. He liked Anjali to a decent extent, talks were nice, sex was good, and they both had their sex bots in case something was missing. They had similar interests, and Rohan especially admired Anjali's honesty. When he asked her why she was leaving, she candidly replied — 'I don't exactly know why. There was a certain attraction in the beginning but now it has faded away.' Rohan realized that honesty is only good as long as it's not hurting. He knew she was right; for him also attraction had reduced, though not as significantly as for her. He still wished to be with her.

In most of Rohan's relationships, things started well but run their course rather quickly. He didn't possess any of the traditional bad qualities such as being possessive, jealous, or uncaring. On the other hand, he didn't have any traditional positive qualities either. With his five-nine height, a physique somewhere between overweight and really fit, hair parted from right to left, and a face easily lost in the crowd, he was a rather average guy. He was not very charming either, conversations with him were not boring but were not long either. With him life was somewhat between exciting and dull. Rohan knew that he lacked qualities that are widely admired, and he wanted to change this, but he also knew that he was set in his ways and cannot be changed.

Rohan arrived at the office and immersed himself in work. He was part of a team assigned with the task of creating robots that humans could genuinely like as friends. Several teams in his office collaborated on this effort. One team focused on humor; machines were fed data from thousands of comedians, books, movies, and people to learn the task of making humans laugh. Humor was considered one of the most challenging qualities for robots to master, but this problem was also solved.

Initially, some robots have filled auditoriums, and have made people roll off their seats. But later just like books this was also banned. And these robots were not bought by anyone for home-use either. Nobody wanted a robot whose comebacks were better than their own. This team was looking into how they can find the right amount of humor as per the individual robot owner and how they can incorporate customizable settings in humor as well.

Another team in the office focused on personality, while yet another concentrated on movements and gestures, and Rohan was working in a team which was making robots learn about human emotions.

Rohan found it rather ironic that he was working in a team working on emotions considering his own shortcomings at emoting. Their team used the principles of sentiment analysis. They had quantified emotions into different categories, these categories were not just actual emotions but were numeric values. Their task was to make machines identify human emotions as a categorized number and respond with an appropriate categorized response. His teams' work was to make machines identify the owner's mood, then identify an appropriate emotional response, then the code from the movement and gestures team would kick in, and the robot would acquire an appropriate expression with the appropriate response.

Rohan's team was working on the problem of optimizing emotional identification. Currently they have an accuracy of 99.7% but their bosses wanted to add as many 9s after the decimal as possible. It was a crucial and reasonable request because one unlike-human response from a machine immediately makes a human conscious that he or she is interacting with a machine. Different members of Rohan's teams were working in pairs on different models to improve this accuracy. Rohan and Ajay had started running a model a few days back to learn from a large pool of human interaction data. And today they are going to test their model on test data. Ajay had high hopes for this model while Rohan as usual was happy with any result, he just wanted to log their teams' findings so that those higher up will know how they have spent their time.

The model took a few hours to run on the test data and finally the results were in. The accuracy of their algorithm turned out to be 99.67%. Ajay angrily bumped the table on which his laptop was resting and exclaimed, "Why don't these machines like me?" Rohan turned towards Ajay and looked at him in surprise. Ajay, a bit annoyed by now, asked, "Why are you looking at me like that?"

"What did you just say?", asked Rohan.

"These machines hate me, why can't they work the way I want?"

"No, repeat your exact statement."

Ajay somewhat irritated reiterated, "What -why don't these machines like me?"

And then it hit Rohan that maybe he cannot make humans like him, but he sure as hell can teach a machine to like him. Until now, the entire AI industry has been focused on making machines that are liked by humans. They didn't realize that one of the basic human needs is not just to like others but to be liked as well. Machines have been made subservient, machines have been made smart and funny, machines have been taught to give responses which humans like. However, no machine has been taught to really like humans.

Rohan was brimming with ideas on how to make a machine crazy in love with him. His mind was coming up with ideas, one after another. He was aware that this would be a substantial project and may take many months to complete, and he may have to go outside the law to achieve what he really wants. It wouldn't be the first time that he would go outside the bounds of the law. Rohan owned two robots, it was a common practice, a lot of people owned multiple robots. Although one robot can manage a considerable amount of work, those who keep multiple robots do it to maintain the illusion of multiple people in their life. One of Rohan's robots looked exactly like his second girlfriend despite the government mandate that robots should not be based on human models other than those which are approved by the authorities.

Though Rohan had been in a few relationships and break-ups after his second break-up, this was the one which had hit him the hardest. What he loved most about his second girlfriend was her love for him. She became crazy for him in a short while and this in turn made him crazy for her. However, over a couple of years her passion for him waned, though his passion didn't. This was the reason that he hit his robot after Anjali dumped him. After getting dumped by Anjali, he was not missing her but was yearning for his second girlfriend. Seeing his robot only intensified that longing.

Initially, people ordered robots based on their loved ones, based on the people they have lost, based on the people they never got. But it was noticed that this caused depression and negative behavior in a lot of robot owners.

Some became fixated on the robots, while some got frustrated on not having the intimacy they expected. Eventually, the government intervened, banning the robots based on specific individuals and instead approved a few thousand models from all walks of life including both real and AI generated faces that didn't resemble any actual humans.

Despite this regulation, Rohan knew of an illegal operation that altered the appearance of robots. From here, he was able to customize his robot to have the desired look.

Another law that Rohan had broken is that individual owners are not allowed to modify or change the algorithms of their robots. Once a company has shipped a robot, the memory containing the base algorithms of a robot was not to be altered. It was like you can save your personal data in the machine without tweaking the operating system. All the algorithms that are shipped in the robots were required to be pre-approved by the government. However, many AI developers who wanted to test their algorithms not just on computers but on actual robots have found a workaround for this restriction.

As soon as Rohan reached his home, he gave a passionate kiss to his robot, envisioning what this robot was going to become. He was on a mission, and the first task at hand was to create a data model and feed it with a significant amount of his personal data. For him, feeding data was not a problem; he possessed thousands of hours of recorded videos and audios, which he has collected to learn, train, and test different algorithms. His plan was to simulate positive emotions in his robot on anything that he said or did, and to simulate negative emotions for things which he didn't like. He even simulated negative emotions even for the things which he liked but couldn't do. His plan was to have a machine which liked, a person who never topped his class but never failed, a person with a bit of humor but not inundated with jokes, a person who can lift a couple of heavy bags but not bench press a truck, a person gets lost in a crowd without turning the eyes of the entire neighborhood.

Rohan continued his office work; he had this new passion and energy that helped him surpass his usual performance. Every evening, he was sitting in front of his computer, even when there was little, he could actively do. Like while his algorithm was learning the desired behavior, he was just checking the logs while imagining how his end-result is going to be. After days of relentless work and numerous optimizations, his algorithm began performing exceptionally well on training data. His algorithm was producing the right results on the data which he had fed to the algorithm to learn. Now came the crucial moment—testing the algorithm on a data it had never encountered before.

He tested the algorithm with some of his audios and videos and the result was as desired; the algorithm responded with positive emotions of varying degrees. Then he tested the algorithm with the data where it was supposed to show negative emotions, this data was not his audios or videos as none of his actions needed to evoke negative emotions. Here his algorithm didn't work well, it was producing neutral emotions for a lot of cases when he was expecting negative. He thoroughly analyzed the failed test cases for a couple of days and realized that actions of people which he had shot personally were yielding inaccurate results. In contrast actions of people from movies and video uploading sites were performing fine.

He realized that videos and audios from movies or even video uploading sites cannot be reliably generalized for real people. Real people rarely behave in a similar way. What he needed was more data, audios, and videos of real people in a non-simulated environment. While he had recordings of his own actions, he lacked data from random strangers.

Rohan's office owned terabytes of data of all types, meticulously categorized in every possible way. However, there was one hiccup for Rohan; he wasn't supposed to take that data for personal use. There were a few safeguards in place to prevent employees from extracting company's intellectual property for personal use. But having worked there for a while Rohan easily figured out how to take data from the office servers to his personal computer.

Now armed with a vast amount of data Rohan could not manually classify, on which data he wanted to simulate positive emotions and on which to simulate negative. He wrote multiple AI based algorithms for this classification, this itself took him a few days. He trained his model again based on the previous data and new data which he acquired. Now his model was performing very close to what he wanted, he kept on re-iterating with different algorithms and different parameters to refine the results further.

Finally, after extensive refactoring and testing, Rohan was satisfied with his work. He ran a final test and results were as per his expectations. He was ready to test his algorithm on his robot. He wiped the memory of his robot clean, not only erasing the accumulated data, but also clearing all the core logic that was inbuilt. He added some of the basic data, which was standard in all robots; information about life on Earth, the utility and purpose of major life forms, and then he added data about self-awareness.

All robots came preloaded with information about their own kind; they have the data that their exterior looks and feels like human beings, but they are different. Their primary purpose of existence was to serve human beings. Rohan deliberately omitted feeding the algorithms related to servitude to his robot. He wanted his algorithms to govern all actions, decisions, and feelings in his robot.

Before shipping, all robots are also fed with data of their owners, and the specific relationship that the robot is expected to have with its owner. Rohan did include information about himself in the robot's data, but deliberately omitted the details about the relation.

Then he added his algorithms to the robot, and after a reboot, his robot was up. He was standing right next to his robot, with his laptop in his hand, a program in his laptop was gauging every action of the robot, dumping a massive log of data. Rohan was intently looking at his robot, and when his robot looked at him, he could feel her emotions change, a change which can only be explained as a release of machine equivalent endorphins. Her eyes were watery, lips were parted, and breathing was shallow. Rohan asked her - "How are you feeling?"

"I don't know, a lot of words are coming to me, but none are matching what's going inside my head" Rohan had tested questions like these while working on his algorithms, but getting this response with change in expression took even him off-guard. While working on his algorithms, Rohan had tested individual statements and responses, but he never tested how a conversation would unfold. He wanted the experience to be new to him as well, and he sought that experience from his robot, not from a computer screen.

Rohan further asked, "Do you know who I am?"

"Of course, I do, you are Rohan, senior developer at GeoUniverse, I know a lot about you."

"And who am I to you?"

"I... I don't know. Who are you to me?"

"Right now, we are just acquaintances, we will be whoever we want to be." She was completely satisfied by this answer, this is exactly the type of things that Rohan would say and the algorithm which was powering her had learned to love. "Can I ask a question if you don't mind?" -Shruti continued.

"Yes, of course. Ask me anything?"

"I know about my kind, but I somehow feel different, why is that?" Rohan was surprised at how quickly she had come to the realization, and he didn't have a completely ready answer for this. "Yes, you are different, all the other robots have a primary drive to serve. Their main task is to follow orders and keep their master" Rohan struggled for a second with the word master and completed the sentence with "owner happy. But you don't have that drive."

"Then what is my primary drive?"

Rohan had not built anything specific as a primary drive, but he knew why he built her. "Your primary drive is love." With a mix of simulations of feelings that were going on inside her head, she was left speechless, having had data from thousands of books, movies, and people, she knew that love is one of the primary forces of the world, and realizing that it was her primary drive made her feel special. She wanted to ask more things, say more things, but words were not coming to her, she just took a deep breath, all the while looking at Rohan with an even more deep admiration and finally asked "What's my name?"

"I used to call you Shruti, I mean not really you, but your body before you were really installed." Rohan was feeling weird using machine related terms for her. "It was the name of someone I knew. But you can pick any name you like."

"I think I will stick with Shruti." Rohan was quite pleased with her decision.

Shruti asked many questions to Rohan, as he had only fed basic information about himself while creating Shruti. She asked Rohan about his work, about his personal life, about his likes/dislikes. Each answer was making her like him even more, and Rohan was loving it. Rohan was not sure what is making her like him more, his words, his voice, his expressions as he has fed all of these to the algorithms which are governing her actions. The machine learning algorithms which he has used were of the type which take thousands of Gigabytes and pass them through various layers, while transforming it on each layer, so that it's hard to visualize or even understand what is happening at each layer. And Rohan was not at all concerned about what was happening at each layer as he was getting the result exactly as he wanted. They kept on talking for the whole night, it was like the best first date that Rohan has ever had. They could have been intimate, but Rohan decided to hold it off, it didn't feel right to him, not just yet.

Next day Rohan took leave from his office to spend time with Shruti. Rohan wanted to catch a movie with her, but he had to be careful that he does not go to any place with metal detectors. Robots do not really need to have any metal inside them but still it was a mandate to add metal in some robot parts so that they can be easily identified. First, they went to a park then a cafe, in the evening Rohan asked her what she wanted to do. The algorithms which were making her like each, and every move of Rohan also made her like the same things as Rohan and she suggested beer and dinner, which made Rohan extremely happy. After they were back, Rohan was wondering should he make a move or is it too soon, by now the thought of her being a robot was not creeping in his mind. He was just happy.

As he was thinking about this, Shruti moved closer to him. She wanted to kiss him but data from hundreds of movies was stopping her from making the first move. Rohan asked her "What do you want to do next?"

"I don't know, what would you like?"

"We can watch a movie together or if you won't mind, maybe... maybe I can kiss you." Rohan knew that the answer to this question didn't directly depend on any algorithm that he had written. He had never fed her any data related to kiss or sex.

"Have you always asked before kissing?"

"No, but you are different from any other girl that I've ever met." Shruti knew she was not a real girl, but it didn't matter to her because it didn't matter to Rohan. She moved and kissed Rohan, first it was slow, then intensity increased, and then they had sex. It was a different experience for Rohan because with previous versions of robots, Rohan knew they couldn't feel anything, their only job was to make their owners happy. But he has fed reinforcement algorithms to Shruti so that she can enjoy sex. This was a very important thing for Rohan; he cannot enjoy things alone, he wanted to give pleasure to others as well. And to achieve this Rohan had made her more passionate even than real humans. While for Shruti this experience was like first sex, and she loved it, every moment of it, every part of it, and she loved Rohan even more.

Next day Rohan went to the office, he had decided that he would not change much of his daily routine to raise any suspicions. He continued his work as if nothing new has happened.

He was loving this phase of his life and wanted things to be as they were for as long as possible. He was doing his work with the same capacity as he was doing earlier. He was keeping his public appearances like hanging out with his friends, office events etc., and the rest of the time he was spending with Shruti. To keep the experience as humane as possible Rohan didn't turn off Shruti while he was out. While Rohan was out, algorithms which were used to design Shruti made her do the things which Rohan would like to do like watching movies, tv shows etc. Rohan did feed data from movies and TV shows while programming, but she still had a lot to catch up. And talking about their favorite TV shows and movies was one of the things they loved to do together. However, merely watching movies or TV shows was not enough for Shruti. She had started studying, studying about Rohan's work, so that she could talk to him like a colleague. Talk about his day, what he did in the office, and how the day went etc.

After a few days like these, Shruti asked Rohan during a casual conversation, "How did your day go?"

"Just the usual, I was working on the same algorithm."

"What algorithm is that?" Rohan was a bit surprised at Shruti's inquisitiveness; she had not asked much about his work before. And he replied -"the usual where we are trying to improve the machine's ability to interpret human emotions." Shruti incisive questions prompted Ajay to ask "Have you been studying AI?"

"Yes, I just wanted to understand what you do."

Ajay beamed pleasantly at her response and explained his work to her in detail, without barring any technicalities. They had quite a fun conversation. For a moment, he thought he would just let Shruti do her work but realized that it's been proven beyond doubt that robots cannot innovate; they can only do what's been already done by humans. Rohan had to improve the efficiency of the emotion identification algorithm, which needs some innovation. Shruti can now write algorithms like the existing ones but cannot put new ideas in them. Still Rohan taught her more; he enjoyed teaching her and even let her do some experiments on his other robot. Soon his other robot kind of became hers.

Shruti continued her routine of watching movies, studying while Rohan was out but she wanted to spend more and more time with Rohan. She used to feel terrible when Rohan had to go out in the evening to office parties, or to outings with friends. She wanted to be out there with Rohan, she wanted to be introduced as his girlfriend.

One night when Rohan was having sex with Shruti, he felt a scar just above her lower back. He touched it more and realized it was quite a big scar. Surprised, he asked "How did you get this?"

"I wanted to remove metal from inside me, I searched for it and it's a straightforward procedure."

"But why?"

"So that I can go out with you."

Ajay looked at her intently, realizing that she couldn't have been killed but she might have felt a lot of pain doing the procedure on her by herself. He checked the site where the procedure was mentioned; it was on the dark web, but it seemed legit to him. Still, before taking her out, he wanted to test it, so he bought a metal detector, scanned her all over multiple times and she was metal-free. Rohan was also extremely excited to take her out, roam all over the country with her, and present her as his girlfriend. But he had to be careful too, so first he took her to a movie. Then let her meet a couple of his close friends whom he can trust. Such that even if they find out, they are just going to reprimand him instead of reporting him in. He decided that his friends Ajay, and Saurabh from the design team were perfect for this.

When meeting his friends, Shruti was both nervous and excited, like a girl in love would be when meeting her boyfriend's friends for the first time. Rohan was quite nervous as well, considering that his friends work in AI and might spot her. But none of them were able to; they were quite impressed by Rohan especially considering how much Shruti was into him. They had some drinks, had dinner and they congratulated both. Ajay told Rohan that now he understands why he was so distracted for the last few days, and that it's okay; he can cover for him in future if required. Rohan had not realized that his distraction had become noticeable, and he made a mental note to not let anyone else notice this.

Gradually, Rohan became even more daring in taking Shruti out. Once he even brought her to an office party. As soon as Shruti entered the event hall, Rohan became extremely tense. The room was filled with hundreds of people from every sector of AI and robotics. Some eyes glanced at her, but none with any doubt. Ajay, Saurabh and some other of Rohan's teammates joined them and they blended into the group. After that Rohan's worry was gone but he still wanted to be cautious. Later at home he asked Shruti to not go out anywhere without him.

A few days later, when Rohan was returning from his office, he went to a cafe near his house, a place he frequented for coffee. As soon as he entered, he spotted Shruti. He was genuinely annoyed with her for being so careless, for being there despite explicitly telling her not to go out anywhere without him.

Approaching her, he asked angrily, "What are you doing here?"

"I just moved back to the city and thought to see you. I knew you would be visiting this cafe on your way back. You haven't changed one bit."

"What?"

"Yeah, I just moved back last week. Don't really know many people here outside work." The realization hit Rohan that he is talking to real Shruti, his ex.

"I know I should have called you first, but I thought let's meet directly." Rohan and Shruti had ended things on friendly terms. Rohan had pretended to be equally nonchalant as Shruti, though he was badly hurt. "No, no it's alright, you can visit me without calling." replied Rohan while coming back to terms with the situation.

"Maybe you can get your coffee and let's go to your house, we can catch up."

"Yeah...no, my house is a bit of a mess right now. Let's catch up here."

They took a seat and talked for a while. All the while Rohan was thinking about the predicament, he was in. Rohan tried to focus on what she was saying, and after a while, he left, excusing himself on pretext of some work.

At home, he discussed this with Shruti, and Rohan asked her to not go out of the house for a while. But she made a request that took Rohan by surprise; she wanted to see the real Shruti. Rohan wondered what part of the algorithms guiding her, would have developed this curiosity. He could not answer that, but he agreed to her request.

In the cafe, Rohan had found out where the real Shruti was living. The next evening, Rohan took Shruti to see her. They waited around an hour near her apartment, and then Shruti saw her for the first time. She felt something for her, she was not sure what it was, it was like a longing, not a longing to be with her, but a longing to be her. For the first time, Shruti regretted that she is not a human. She noticed Rohan looking at the real Shruti, there was a sparkle in his eyes, she had seen that sparkle in his eyes many times when he saw her. She realized that he still likes her, she wondered if Rohan likes her more, or for him both, she and the real Shruti were the same.

When they reached back, Shruti asked Rohan tons of questions about Shruti. And Rohan shared a lot of information, how they met, how they fell for each other, what they used to do when they were together. Shruti loved hearing these stories; she wanted to know each and everything about the real Shruti. They spent the entire night talking about her.

Rohan returned to his normal schedule, going to the office, hanging out with colleagues for the sake of appearances, and spending the rest of the time with Shruti. Rohan had asked Shruti to not go out anymore, and she agreed. They talked about various things, including what she had learned, things she still didn't know, things that surprised her, movies they watched, and songs they liked. Sometimes Rohan even let her assist with some of his work.

On a weekend when Rohan was hanging out with Shruti, he heard a knock on his door, he looked through the peephole and it was Shruti. He was shocked and didn't move for a moment and then told Shruti about the visitor and asked her to hide inside.

He opened the door, and Shruti was fuming, Rohan can feel rage emanating from her. She was hyperventilating, her eyes were red. Before he could ask anything Shruti blurted out "How could you?"

"How could I - what?"

"Don't you dare act coy with me. I met your friend, and he told me everything. That you have been dating me for a while, though I am just back in the city."

"Alright, I am really sorry, I wanted to tell you but..."

"How could you do that Rohan, despite knowing how many laws you have broken. How and why?"

"I just, I don't know, I wanted to be with you." Rohan knew that he was only telling the partial truth; this might have been true earlier, but after he created Shruti, he hadn't even thought about her.

Shruti mellowed out a little and said, "I want to see her."

"What, why?"

"Because... She is me or my replica."

"Ok, wait a second."

Rohan called Shruti from inside, she came out a little sheepishly. She stole a glance at Shruti, she was not able to meet her eyes. She had seen her, but this was the first time she was meeting her; she thought, 'So this is the person on whom I am based, I am the replica, and she is the original'. While other Shruti was eyeing her from top to bottom. She realized that Rohan has focused on making their faces the same but had not focused on all the aspects. Even their heights differ, but by an inch only. And with both having average build no one could tell them apart.

A few minutes ago, Shruti was adamant on meeting her replica but right now she was at loss of words. She opened her mouth to say something, but words didn't come out and she hurried out of the house. Rohan followed her outside. She had not gone too far from his gate; she was waiting for him to come out. Inside, Shruti was having her ears on the door trying to listen to what's going on outside and she heard Shruti's voice" I want her destroyed."

"What, why?" Rohan protested.

"What do you mean why? You have no right to keep a robot just like me. If you were still in love with me, you could have come to me. I know we got separated but we could have been united again; my feelings for you were not dead. But with you doing what you have done, I am feeling replaceable, I am feeling violated."

Rohan might have initially based his robot's face on her out of some residual feelings. However, when he implemented the algorithms governing his robot, he was not thinking of her at all. But he realized this is not the right time to share that information, and he said to her, "If you have problems with her looks, I will change it, I will not even take the human models; I will take one of those AI-generated faces which do not resemble any human on earth."

"No, it's not just her face anymore. You have created her after me, and I will always know that. I am coming tomorrow, and we are going to take her to a junkyard and get her destroyed, I will accompany you to the junkyard. You have one day to say your goodbyes."

Rohan wanted to argue but she just ran off to her car and left.

Rohan was not sure what to do; he just stood there on his gate for a while, afraid to go inside. He wasn't sure what to say to Shruti and how to say it. After some hesitation, he entered, took one look at Shruti, and realized she had heard everything. He said immediately, "Don't worry, I will not let her destroy you. Just give me some time to think." Rohan wanted to think of how to save Shruti and he went inside his room, leaving her alone.

After spending more than a couple of hours inside, Rohan returned and found Shruti sitting with his other robot. He asked his other robot to leave, then hugged Shruti and said – "I am downloading all your memories and intelligence in a drive, and I will systematically erase today's events. And load the remaining data and intelligence in a different robot with different appearance."

"Wouldn't the new me wonder why I have a different face than my memories?"

"I'll have an explanation for that which you wouldn't mind at all. Trust me."

"But you like this face, don't you? And you would know the difference."

"No, I don't like this face. I mean I do but it's you, what's inside you that matters."

"And what's that a mesh of 1s and 0s?"

"What do you think is inside my brain or any human's brain? It's electrical signals, just like yours."

"I know you love me Rohan, I love you too, and I love you like a human. So, there is another thing which I would like to do like humans; die once only. I want you to remember me as your lover, as a lover whom you lost, not as your creation. I know you could create me again, but please don't do it, it will not be as good. Your mind will compare, and it will never be as good as what we had. I want you to promise me Rohan, that you would destroy all your work and you will never try to recreate me."

Rohan was silent, a tear trickled from his left eye, and he made the promise that Shruti was seeking.

Rohan and Shruti spent a solemn night together. There was talking, hugging, kissing, they hadn't planned for it, but they did have sex for one last time. They reminisced about their favorite moments, Shruti remembered the first time she leaned on his shoulder. They were sitting on a couch in a rooftop bar, it was a cold day, she was wearing a sleeveless top, she rested her head on his shoulder. She realized that his hand on which she was leaning was not comfortable and she just lifted it around her neck and put it on the side of her other shoulder, he held her shoulder, and pulled her closer to him, very close and kissed her forehead – an episode etched in Rohan's heart.

Together they remembered some other times, the first time they had drinks together, the first time they had sex, and many other moments which they spent together. Rohan had a habit of recording videos and taking photos of a lot of moments, they watched some of them. As the morning was approaching, they couldn't watch any more videos, they couldn't talk or sleep either, they just stayed in each other's arms till the first light of dawn.

Shruti was outside Rohan's house at eleven, she didn't even come inside. Rohan came out in a while, an expressionless blank Shruti walking right next to him. He had deactivated the part of her system running most algorithms, all she had was some basic motions. He sat on the front seat next to Shruti and asked his robot to sit in the back. Shruti punched in the location of the nearest bot scrapyard in her car GPS, there was only one in the vicinity. As they reached the place, Rohan and Shruti were greeted by another robot whose sole purpose was to evaluate the incoming robots and pay the owners accordingly. A robot in charge of destroying other robots. The scrapping industry salvaged useful components, recycled whatever possible, and disposed of the rest. Owner gets something in return for their bot which Rohan didn't want, but the bots at front were supposed to pay the owner, and Rohan knew not accepting money might not be programmed in them. In case robot owner and processing robot don't come to an agreement, human manager of the shop intervenes, which Rohan didn't want. He took whatever they offered and left without even collecting a bill of sale.

Rohan remained distraught throughout the journey back. Shruti's anger had subsided, she attempted to engage him in conversation, he remained unresponsive. Upon reaching his home, he simply disembarked and headed inside without uttering a word.

He was not able to place anything -'How did it happen? What will he do now?' He locked himself in a room, slept, cried, threw some things around. Thought of re-creating Shruti, then he remembered his promise to Shruti. A part of his mind said to him you don't need to bother about your promise to her, she was just a bot. And the thought filled him with uncontrollable guilt, another part of his mind took over and shouted at him, that she was not just a robot, she was everything and you will respect her wishes.

His other robot took care of basic needs like feeding him, he ate just the minimal and sometimes not even that. He had taken a week's leave during which he moped endlessly. Eventually a part of his mind decided that he will get back to work and will keep on dredging like he used to do. He decided that he will survive and that's it, he didn't want to do anything else. He got back into his lifestyle and got back to his usual habits. He was much more sullen, dull, and sad. He told his friends that he and Shruti had broken-up. His friends attributed his behavior to breaking up with Shruti and hoped that he would get back to his normal self soon. A couple of months passed by and his current self, became his new normal.

On a Thursday on his way back from office Rohan saw Shruti entering the cafe he frequented. He shook his head thinking his mind is playing tricks with him. He went inside the cafe and there she was calmly sitting at a table, sipping coffee. It took a moment for Rohan to realize she's not his robot, she's the actual Shruti. A burst of anger surged in his mind, he charged at her table, "What the hell are you doing here?"

Shruti looked up, "Just wanted to see how you are doing."

"Seen enough? You may go now."

"You still think I did wrong?"

"You killed her."

"I did it for you."

"What?" snapped Rohan.

"Yes, there were two of me, Rohan. You were bound to get caught sooner or later."

"I could have changed the way she looked."

"I just wanted to show it to you that you didn't need her, but if you really want to, can't you create her again. I won't stop you this time."

"Didn't need her, she's the only thing I ever needed. And I can't recreate her; she didn't want me to."

"Rohan, I thought that once she is gone, maybe you would realize you don't need her. But I was wrong, and I am sorry for that. And there was another reason I wanted her to be gone."

"Yeah, what's that?" Rohan was having hard time controlling his anger.

"I thought maybe we could be together."

"You're crazy. Stay away from me." Rohan left the cafe disgusted by her.

After a couple of days Rohan saw Shruti again at the cafe. He didn't go to her; she didn't approach him either and Rohan took off after taking his coffee. This became their usual routine. After weeks of receiving cold shoulder from Rohan, Shruti accosted him just outside the cafe and said, "I want one date."

"No, I can't, you will always remind me of her."

"Would you prefer that I keep bumping into you every day here or you spend some time with me on one date?" A part of Rohan was liking this new behavior of Shruti.

There was something different about her. But still, what she had made him do to his Shruti, was not allowing him to have any positive feelings towards her. "Alright one meeting but after that you will never come up here or anywhere near my house or office."

Shruti arranged for them to meet at a pub. It was a nice cozy little place, divided into sections, where people were supposed to sit on cushions on a raised platform, with a small concrete structure in front acting as a table. Each section can accommodate up to eight people. Shruti had booked one section just for Rohan and her. Rohan sat in front of her and asked - "Couldn't you have booked a place where I could have kept my shoes on while sitting?"

"Still grumpy, are we?"

"You have taken something that was most precious to me, and you think I can forget that over a beer."

"No, not over one beer but maybe around three." Shruti said sheepishly.

This did bring a momentary smile on Rohan's face, and that smile led to anger, "I am not having any drinks, I just want to get it over with."

"That's not fair, you promised me a date and I know how much you like to drink on dates."

"And how much is that?"

"Enough to boost your confidence but not enough to make a fool out of you. So at least a couple of beers."

"Alright but two beers and then I am gone. After that you are out of my life, and I can try to forget her."

Rohan finished his first beer quite quickly, and ordered his second, the moment he ordered his second, Shruti got up from her seat and sat next to him, leaned on him and put her head on his shoulders and asked, "Remember the first time I did this?"

"What?" Rohan was confused.

"Leaned on your shoulder, and then I put your arm around me and put it on the side of my shoulder and you pulled me towards you and…"

"Kissed your forehead. How do you know about this? I never did it with you or anybody else, I did it just with Shruti, my Shruti."

"I am your Shruti."

"What, what are you talking about?"

"It was either her or me, I chose me."

"You… you killed her."

"Or she would have gotten me killed."

"But how?"

Shruti explained to Rohan how she had asked his other robot to come to the junkyard and pay for her, and buy her back. She had removed the metallic parts from him as well. She stayed in a hotel near Shruti's apartment and observed her, went to her house in her absence, and downloaded all the information about her from her robot and her social media accounts. She even learned about her job, and then finally, she got rid of her. She didn't share any details of how. She asked. - "Are you mad at me?"

"Mad! No, I am not mad at you. You get mad when someone drops a cup of tea or cuts you in traffic. But when someone murders a person, you get repulsed, you get horrified."

"Are you... are you repulsed by me?"

"I don't know what I am feeling. Maybe I need some time to find out what I am feeling."

"Do you think this is our last date?"

"I don't know, I will call you in a while. For now, I just want to leave."

"Alright, I will wait for your call, I just want to say one more thing. I did this for us. I couldn't bear the thought of either of us living without the other person." Saying this, she left.

Rohan was alone with his thoughts. But his thoughts were betraying him. He wanted to feel guilty, sad, horrified but he was not feeling any of those things if anything he was feeling relieved. He wanted to blame himself for what had happened; it was his creation which had done the deed, but he couldn't. All he could think of was how happy he was when he was with her, and how miserable he was for the last few months. He had concluded that Shruti had taken the only rational choice available to her and even before it hit dawn, he called her and asked her to come back. It took him some time to completely forget about what had happened, but he did forget.

In a few months Rohan and Shruti were living together. Both of their friends knew about their committed status.

They had thought of getting married, but the idea of having all their friends and relatives, especially Shruti's, scared them to drop the idea. Shruti had quit her job and had also reduced her already limited interactions with her friends and family in case something slipped out. Everyone attributed these changes as a new chapter of her life which she was starting with Rohan. And Rohan and Shruti were both extremely happy. Every moment they spent together was like a blessing. Shruti loved everything that Rohan did, and Rohan was loving that love. Other than Rohan's office hours, they were spending every minute together. Almost every night was like a date, drinking beer, wine, scotch, and eating extravagant food. After a while this behavior started taking a toll on Rohan's health.

He started to cut back on these activities, but with the reduction of these activities, the duration of their conversation, which was already declining, decreased even further. The absence of alcohol and multi-course meals cut the time they used to spend together. Even Rohan's interests changed, from action and adventure or comedies he moved to documentaries and short films. Shruti gave company to Rohan, but she was not enjoying that time. She was unable to understand why, despite having a primary drive to love Rohan, she is not enjoying her time with him. And Rohan was oblivious to these things. During this time his attitude of satisfied with being average at work also changed, he wanted to excel. He wanted to go places along with Shruti, wanted to do things which cost money and for that he started working hard and spending even less time with Shruti. Their frequency of getting intimate also reduced.

When Rohan was away Shruti started watching old tapes of Rohan; tapes like that Rohan had used in creating the algorithms running her. Those tapes filled her up with feelings of love. She loved every second of those videos. One day after watching a video of their old date, she was filled with love and wanted to relive that. She prepared a meal with all of Rohan's favorites, she cooked up some grilled chicken, prawns starters and a chicken curry. She set the table with some starters and a couple of beers, wore a dress which Rohan loved, and as the clock was about to strike seven, she sat on a chair, with her eyes on the gate and a smile on her face.

However, Rohan was late, even by nine o' clock he didn't arrive, she didn't mind. She was still in her state of ecstasy. Finally, she heard the door opening. A tired-looking Rohan entered, he looked at her, gave her a meek smile, and went to his room to freshen up. When he came back, he kissed her on the cheek, looked at the table and said, "Aww, I wish you had told me you were preparing all these things, I had some really heavy evening snacks; I can't eat much now. Maybe just a little salad or rice, that's it. Also, please put the beer back, maybe we can have it at some other time."

For the first time Shruti felt totally sad, she had felt odd before but something or other from his behavior used to cheer her up. However, how he behaved today was unlike anything he used in her programming. She said, "Earlier you used to keep on taking pint after pint from the fridge just so that you could spend some more time with me, and now you don't want to have even one."

"Well yeah, I ate a lot in the evening; if I drink now, it will upset my stomach. If only you would have told me in the evening."

"Earlier you didn't use to care that about your stomach."

"Yeah, but people change. And not just in one way, every aspect of them changes." As soon as Rohan said that he realized, that's what he had not considered, he hadn't programmed Shruti to love the changes happening in him. He will need to tweak her algorithms and enable continuous learning in her, so that she can keep on loving every aspect of his personality including the changes. He said to her, "I am sorry, at least I should have let you know that I was eating in the office." And he hugged her, Shruti was not completely appeased, but she hugged him back.

Rohan had started work on changes in Shruti's algorithms. This time, he was not as passionate as he was the first time while writing algorithms for Shruti. He was taking it slow, procrastinating a lot, but after having a few more arguments, he got more focused. Also, this time around, he was not freely working at home, as he wanted to do this without Shruti finding out. He used to work on it mostly from the office and this led him to spend even more time at the office.

Finally, after a couple of months he was ready to test these new algorithms on Shruti. Rohan reached home early and opened the door. He could not find Shruti in the hall. As he approached his bedroom, he heard Shruti's voice, and there was another voice, a man's voice, quite familiar. He went inside the room and saw a man, he was facing opposite to the door, looking towards Shruti. Shruti looked at Rohan smilingly, confused Rohan asked, "Who is he?"

"He is you" replied Shruti, and the other person turned towards him having the same face as his.

Rohan was taken aback, he realized, it's his other robot, whom Shruti had got redesigned to look like him, his curiosity took him forward to examine the robot closely. He was surprised but he was feeling a hint of admiration for Shruti's work. His robot moved away and stood a little back behind Rohan to let Rohan and Shruti talk. Rohan said to Shruti, "I am so sorry love, I have been spending so much time in the office, from now on I will be spending more time with you. But it's fine if you would like him to accompany you when I am not here." Rohan said that though he was not completely sure about this. He didn't want to share his Shruti.

"It's not that I mind you going to office, I've not created him to accompany me while you are gone to office."

"Then why have you created him?"

"Because like you he will not change. We will both stay the same forever."

"Are you planning to leave me?" Shock ran across Rohan's face. "I will not be able to live without you, what will happen to me?"

Shruti looked at Rohan lovingly and said, "I guess, same as what happened to Shruti."

Rohan felt a sudden, hard blow to the back of his head. He stumbled forward, disoriented, trying to make sense of what just happened. Shruti's voice sounded distant as she said, "I couldn't bear the thought of either of us living without the other person."

As his vision blurred, Rohan saw the two faces—one his own, the other Shruti's. He collapsed to the floor, consciousness slipping away. Shruti stood over him, her expression a mix of love and a cold determination.

The room faded into darkness as Rohan lost consciousness.

www.ingramcontent.com/pod-product-compliance
Lightning Source LLC
LaVergne TN
LVHW061623070526
838199LV00078B/7399